The Conflict Resolution Library™

Dealing with Someone Who Is Selfish

• Don Middleton •

The Rosen Publishing Group's
PowerKids Press™
New York

This book is dedicated to my wife, Sue; my daughters, Jody and Kim; my mother-in-law, Mim; and my parents, Bernice and Helmut Bischoff. Also, special thanks to authors and friends Diana Star Helmer and Tom Owens for believing in me. —Don Middleton

Published in 1999 by The Rosen Publishing Group, Inc.
29 East 21st Street, New York, NY 10010

Photo Credits and Photo Illustrations: p. 4 © Scott Campbell/International Stock; p. 7 © Giovanni Lunardi/International Stock; p. 8 © Jeff Kaufman/FPG International; p. 11 by Thomas Mangieri; p. 12 © Jacob Taposchaner/FPG International; p. 15 © Bill Tucker/International Stock; p. 16 by Guillermina de Ferrari; p. 19 by Seth Dinnerman; p. 20 © Robin Schwartz/International Stock.

First Edition

Layout and design: Erin McKenna

Middleton, Don.
    Dealing with someone who is selfish / by Don Middleton.
        p.   cm.—(The conflict resolution library)
    Includes index.
    Summary: Discusses the nature and effects of selfishness and how to deal with someone who is selfish.
    ISBN 0-8239-5268-1
    1. Selfishness—United States—Juvenile literature. 2. Sharing—United States—Juvenile literature. [1. Selfishness. 2. Sharing.] I. Title. II. Series.
    BJ1535.S4M53 1998
    179'.8—dc21   98-5641
                                                                                          CIP
                                                                                          AC

Manufactured in the United States of America

Contents

Being Selfish

Selfishness (SEL-fish-nus) means keeping things for yourself instead of sharing with others. Selfish kids might not let you join in a game they're playing. A selfish friend might bring something in to show the class, but won't let you touch it. There are many reasons why people act selfishly. One of the biggest reasons is that some kids don't feel good about themselves. These kids think being selfish will make them feel better. But it doesn't.

◄ *Some kids know happiness can come from sharing.*

Giving of Yourself

As you grow up, the people around you teach you to share. A parent may help you make a birthday card to give to a special friend. A classmate might offer to help you with your homework. Sharing sometimes means giving of yourself and your time. Some kids may not have learned enough about sharing, so they behave selfishly.

Sharing time with a brother or sister can make you both feel good. ▶

The Basketball Game

The school bell rang for morning recess.
Tom hurried to the basketball court.
"Hey, can I play, too?" asked Tom.
"Can't you see? We've already got enough players!" one of the boys shouted.
"Hold on," said Bill. "Tom can play on our team. We'll just take turns."
After the game, the boys returned to class.
Tom said to Bill, "Thanks for giving me a chance."
"That's okay. You always give other kids a chance to play," Bill answered.

◀ *Sharing with others can make you feel good about yourself.*

9

Express Your Feelings

When someone acts in a selfish way toward you, try not to get angry. Getting angry won't help. And yelling at the person may only lead to a fight.

Instead, talk to people in a calm and gentle way. Try to explain to others how it makes you feel when they act selfishly. Let people who are being selfish know how much more fun things can be when people share.

It is important to express yourself to your friends. ▶

Listening

Telling someone how her selfish **behavior** (bee-HAY-vyur) makes you feel is only the beginning. Chances are your friend will offer an excuse for selfish behavior. As your friend explains her behavior, stay quiet and try to understand how she feels. Even if your friend gets angry as she speaks, make sure you stay calm and **focused** (FOH-kisd). Being a good listener is part of being a good friend.

◀ *Talking about sharing is teaching about sharing.*

The Internet

After lunch, Erica went to the computer. It was her turn on the **Internet** (IN-ter-net). But Nancy was already using the computer.

"I need to use that computer," Erica said.

"There are other computers! I'm writing a long e-mail," Nancy replied.

"But that's the only one with Internet **access** (AK-ses). And it's my turn today," Erica said calmly.

"Oh! I didn't know that," Nancy said. "I'll write this e-mail later."

Sharing allows everyone a chance to use things. ▶

Talking Things Out

Sometimes people won't share their time because they can't. By talking with someone about why he won't help you, you may find out that he has a good reason. Your brother wouldn't trade chores with you? He wasn't being selfish. He had to go to soccer practice. A classmate wouldn't help you move your desk? It turns out she was doing homework she hadn't finished. Ask people in a nice way why they can't help or share. Talking things out can help you understand their reasons.

◀ *Helping out at home is one way to share your time.*

When Nothing Works

Sometimes talking to a selfish friend doesn't work. The friend may not seem to care how you feel. Or the friend might not want to explain how he or she feels. If this happens, give your friend time. Maybe he or she will feel differently later on.

Remember, you don't have to act selfishly just because others around you do. You can still set a good example for others. A selfish friend might watch you and decide that it is more fun to share.

You can share time and fun with friends ▶
even if others behave selfishly.

The Assignment

Josh needed to finish his project. The school librarian told him the book he needed was overdue. Josh's classmate Percy had not returned the book.

"Percy, do you have a library book that's past due?" Josh asked.

"Why do you care?" Percy asked.

"I need that book for my project," he said.

"I'll return it whenever I want," Percy yelled. Josh felt bad. He called his mother. Josh's mom said she'd drive him to another library after school. He could get the book there.

◀ *Josh felt bad, but he found another answer to his problem.*

The Joys of Sharing

We all have acted selfishly at some time in our lives. Whether we meant to or not, it probably didn't make us feel good about ourselves. But it usually feels good to share. You can share your toys or books. Taking turns on the swings is also sharing. Sharing lets you have fun with others. It helps you make new friends and feel good about yourself.

Glossary

access (AK-ses) To be able to connect with or get to something.

behavior (bee-HAY-vyur) How a person acts.

focus (FOH-kis) Concentration.

Internet (IN-ter-net) An electronic network that connects computers around the world.

selfish (SEL-fish) Being more concerned about yourself than about others.

Index